Tonka®
WORKING HARD WITH THE MIGHTY MIXER™

Written by Francine Hughes
Illustrated by Steven James Petruccio

SCHOLASTIC INC.
New York   Toronto   London   Auckland   Sydney

The editors would like to thank Michael Thompson for all of his help.

ISBN 0-590-47308-5

Copyright © 1993 by Tonka Corporation.
All rights reserved. Published by Scholastic Inc., by arrangement with Tonka Corporation, 1027 Newport Avenue, Pawtucket, RI 02862.
MIGHTY TONKA is a trademark of Tonka Corporation.

12 11 10 9 8 7 6 5 4 3 2   3 4 5 6 7 8/9

Printed in the U.S.A.   24

First Scholastic printing, November 1993

Mike drives a Mighty Mixer. His job is to bring
concrete to construction sites. Each morning
Mike goes to the plant where concrete is made.

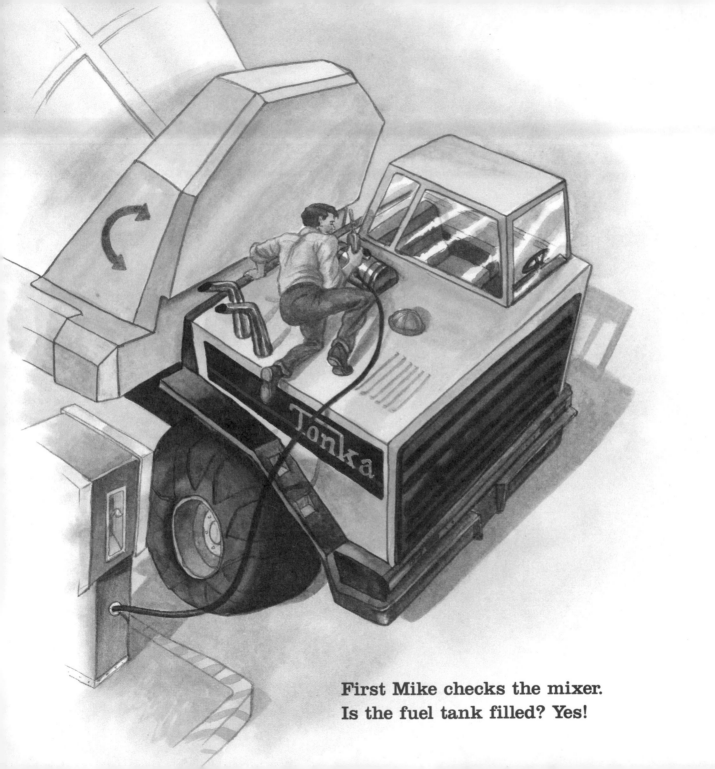

First Mike checks the mixer.
Is the fuel tank filled? Yes!

Do the tires need air? No! The Mighty Mixer
is ready to go.

Mike drives the Mighty Mixer under a tower called a batch plant. Cement, sand, gravel, and water are all mixed together inside. Out pours the wet, heavy concrete — right into the mixer's drum!

But the concrete isn't ready yet! It needs
more mixing. Mike pulls a lever inside the
mixer's cab. *Whir. Whir.* The drum starts
to turn.

It keeps turning and mixing, mixing and turning as Mike drives to the construction site — an elementary school.

Rat-a-tat-tat! Rat-a-tat-tat! Jackhammers
are breaking up parts of the old school
yard. A loader carries away the rubble.

Then the workers build a form. They place strips
of wood around the school yard. This form will
hold the concrete in place until it hardens.
Once the form is ready, Mike's job begins.

Mike lowers the chute at the back of the
Mighty Mixer. Then he pulls another lever
inside the cab. *Whir. Whir.* Now the drum
is turning the other way.

Concrete pours out of the truck,
down the chute, and into place.

A worker smooths out
the concrete.

When it dries,
the wooden form will
be removed.

Then schoolchildren will be able to play
in the brand-new school yard.

Later in the week, Mike is on his way
to help build an apartment building.
First, backhoes and dump trucks get
the site ready.

They dig, dig, dig the dirt. Then they
haul it away. Again and again the
trucks do their jobs until the hole in
the ground is wide and even.

Now it's time for the foundation. Everything else will be built on top of that. Mike starts by pouring some concrete into a wheelbarrow. He realizes the mixture needs water. It's easy to add — the Mighty Mixer has its very own water tank.

Once again the drum spins round and round.
This time the concrete is just right.
It comes pouring out of the mixer. Soon it
fills the hole. The foundation is made.
Mike's job is finished.

Back at the plant, Mike washes down the
Mighty Mixer. Then he pours water into
the drum, and the truck churns the water
out — just like it's concrete.

Now the Mighty Mixer is clean inside
and out, and ready for work tomorrow.

Mike's next job is to help build a highway.
He drives along a bumpy dirt road to begin work.
Big dump trucks and other machines are already
there, doing their part to clear the way.

Once the dirt road is ready, Mike's job begins. The concrete is poured as the Mighty Mixer moves along. Right behind the mixer is a spreading machine, working to smooth out the bumps.

After the concrete has dried and the road
has been paved, people will have a new
highway — and a faster way to get to the city.

Today Mike's job is to help build a new airline terminal in the middle of a busy airport.

There are lots of other mixers at the site. Each truck pours its load into a different part of the foundation to make the job go more quickly.

Bit by bit, the building grows taller and taller. The Mighty Mixer helps make heavy slabs of concrete.

Then the cranes lift these heavy slabs
up to the top floor of the building.
This airline terminal is made mostly of
steel and concrete.

Mike likes working with the Mighty Mixer.
He is always busy. His next job might
be to help make concrete blocks for a tunnel . . .

. . . or to help pour the concrete beams for a bridge.

Mike and the Mighty Mixer might pour
the foundation for a movie theater . . .

. . . or add a new ramp to a skateboard park!

Mike enjoys doing many different jobs.
That's why he likes driving the
Mighty Mixer!